How the Hibernators
Came to Bethlehem

How the Hibernators Came to Bethlehem

by Norma Farber
Illustrated by Barbara Cooney

Walker and Company ✺ New York, New York

Library of Congress Cataloging in Publication Data

Farber, Norma.
    How the hibernators came to Bethlehem.
    SUMMARY: The Star of Bethlehem awakens the winter-
sleeping creatures, such as Bear, Badger, and Raccoon,
to send them to visit a newborn baby.
    [1. Christmas stories]   I. Cooney, Barbara,
1917-   II. Title.
PZ7.F2228Ho 1980   [E]   80-7685
ISBN 0-8027-6352-9
ISBN 0-8027-6353-7 lib. bdg.

First published in the United States of America in 1980
by the Walker Publishing Company, Inc.

Tr. ISBN 0-8027-6352-9   Reinf. ISBN 0-8027-6353-7
Library of Congress Catalog Card Number 80-7685
Printe in the United States of America
10   9   8   7   6   5   4   3   2   1

This story was written
for Helen Margaret by Norma Farber.
These pictures were drawn
for Sammy by Granny.

Once upon a winter's night two thousand years ago,
a star shone,
so far, so strong,
it woke every winter-sleeping creature.

Bear was the first to stir.
The heaviest hibernator slept lightest of all.
He only snoozled, really, a kind of cat-nap.
He lay groggy on the north side of a mountain.
In the starlight he looked a great black cushion
such as giants might rest their heads on.

Every hair glistened like patent leather.
The star poked at him with a dainty silver wand,
through fat at least four inches thick.
He stretched and yawned.
The star sang down to him, *Bethlehem*!

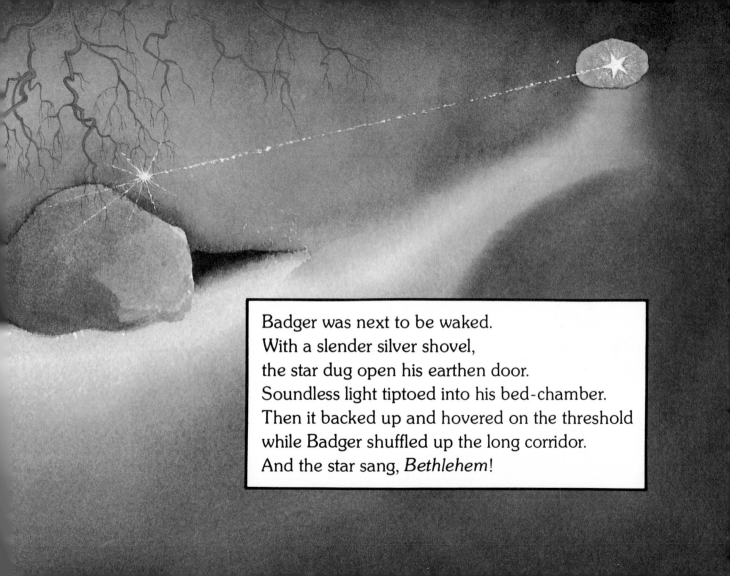

Badger was next to be waked.
With a slender silver shovel,
the star dug open his earthen door.
Soundless light tiptoed into his bed-chamber.
Then it backed up and hovered on the threshold
while Badger shuffled up the long corridor.
And the star sang, *Bethlehem*!

In nearby dens
Skunk and Raccoon were huddled motionless.
The star inserted a silver pass-key,
first at one keyhole, then at the other.
The locks of the hiding-places sprang open.
Skunk and Raccoon shook themselves.
They followed slumbrously where they were led,
as their star sang, *Bethlehem*!

It was Tortoise's turn next.
Starlight flicked open a breathing-space
in the swampy ground near his head.
Slowly, in his heavy suit of armor,
Tortoise pushed himself out of mud and mire
to where the star was singing, *Bethlehem*!

Ground Squirrel, you're next! Wake up!
Oh yes, these dried grasses are soft,
this circular den is cozy,
buried seeds and bulbs so tasty.
But a star has alighted on your lintel,
twirling a wand like a baton.
Time to toddle up the burrow,
to hear how brightly the star sings, *Bethlehem*!

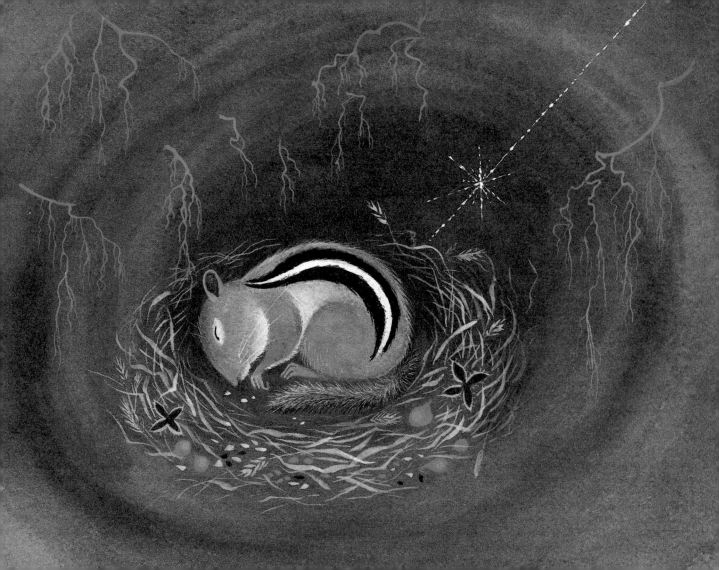

And now the star hovered over Bat
as he turned rightside up under the eave
where he had been hanging upside down.
For he had been resting only fitfully.
A breath of fresh air, he thought,
should help me fall asleep.

A silver feather tapped him between the eyes.
He sneezed so loud the star twinkled.
He stretched his full length,
and spread out his full breadth,
alert and curious to hear the star sing, *Bethlehem*!
Follow me to Bethlehem!

In short order
the star sang every winter-sleeping creature awake—
  Bird,
          Mammal,
                  Reptile,
                          Amphibian,
                                  Fish,
                                      Insect.

In no time at all they came to a manger.
There Lion and Lamb and dozens of other animals
were already gathered close.
They were watching a newborn baby in a mound of sweet hay.

Three Kings were there also,
kneeling.
"Look!" said the Kings.
"Even the hibernators have come!"

And everyone was very quiet, listening, while the star sang on and on, *Bethlehem*!

And on and on and on, *Bethlehem*!